SATO
THE RABBIT
THE MOON

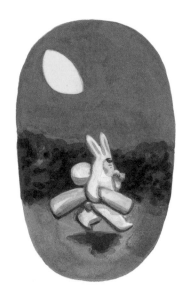

YUKI AINOYA
TRANSLATED FROM JAPANESE
BY MICHAEL BLASKOWSKY

Enchanted Lion Books
NEW YORK

One bright evening,

the moon sinks into
a western forest.

Haneru Sato the Rabbit
goes into the woods
and pulls the moon out
from a thicket.

Where is Sato going today
in his moon boat?

THE GREEN SCREW

Sato the Rabbit walks into
a meadow.

It's a perfect day for turning
a screw in a field.

He discovers a green screw
hidden amidst the dry grass,

and turns it slowly.
When he does…

Sato continues to slowly
turn the screw.

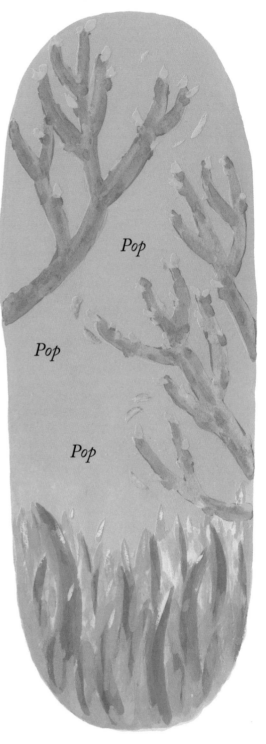

Now surrounded
by green, Sato finds
a handle.

And when he slowly
turns the handle...

there's a shower
of green.

FLOWER BASKET

Deep in the forest, there's a patch
of trees in bloom.

Sato the Rabbit finds a tree that
fits him perfectly and sits down.

It smells wonderful underneath the blooming tree.

All Sato can see above him are flowering branches.

Petals are scattered across the ground.

Night falls and the stars appear.
The blooming branches become even more fragrant.

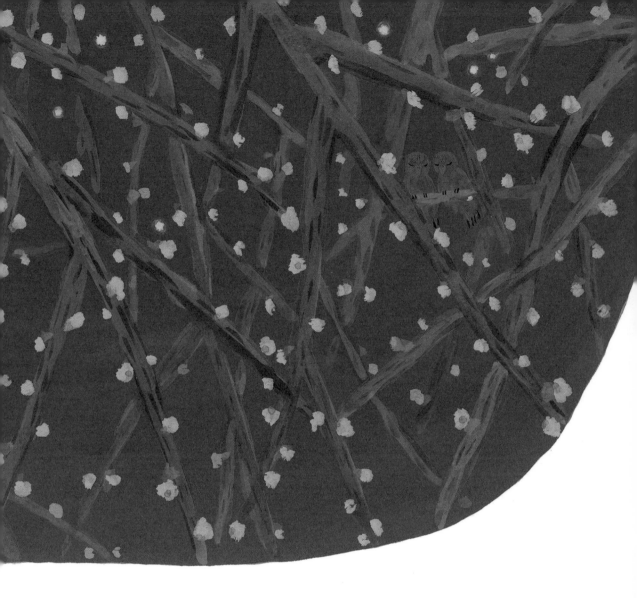

Enveloped in that lovely scent,
Sato begins to feel a little sleepy.

And when he does...

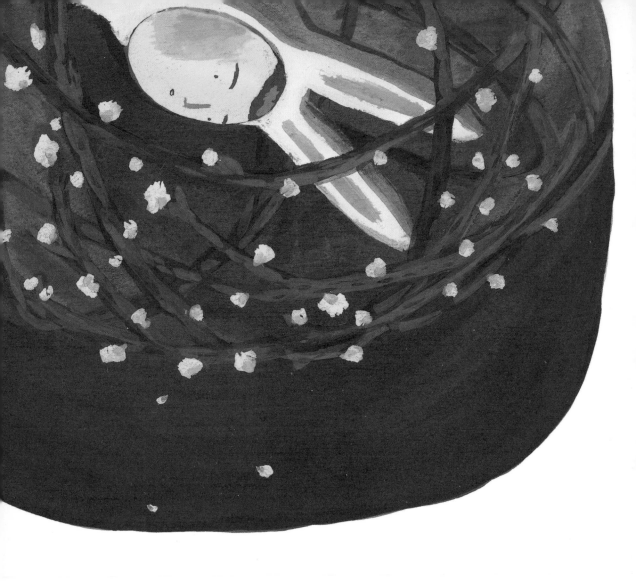

the flowery branches wrap around Sato and rise gently into the air.

And for a while, everyone enjoys the spring night sky. 🌷

FALLING RAIN

It looks like it will rain today.

Sato the Rabbit gets ready for a rain party.

First, the music.

Next, a specially made ribbon.

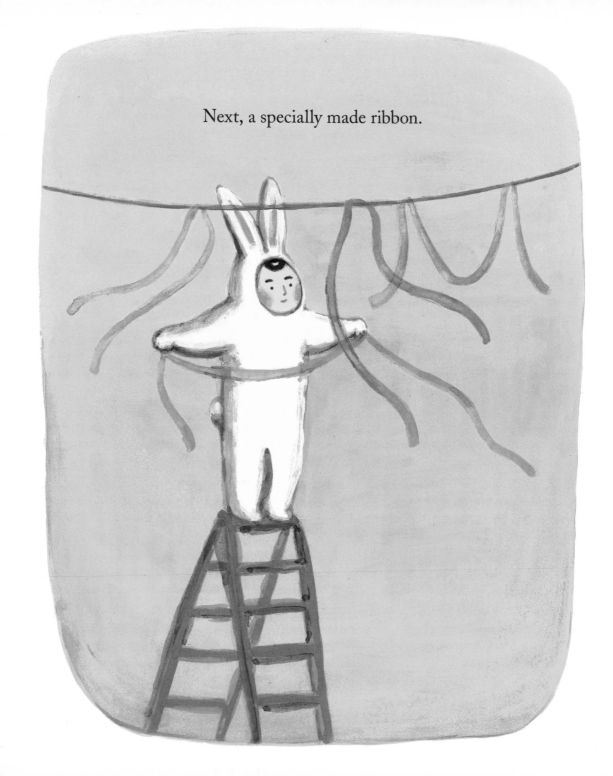

The rain arrives.

Drip drop
Plink plonk
Splitter splatter splash

Sato ties
the rain
with ribbon.

Boom boom
Tink-a-tink tink
Bum ba-dum bum
Rain music echoes through
the rain-column ballroom.

SPRING WATER

One especially hot afternoon, Sato the Rabbit cools his feet in a cold spring.

Still hot,
he cools his ears next.

Burble burble
It's so very quiet
under the water.

Burble burble
The bubbling of the water
is the only sound.

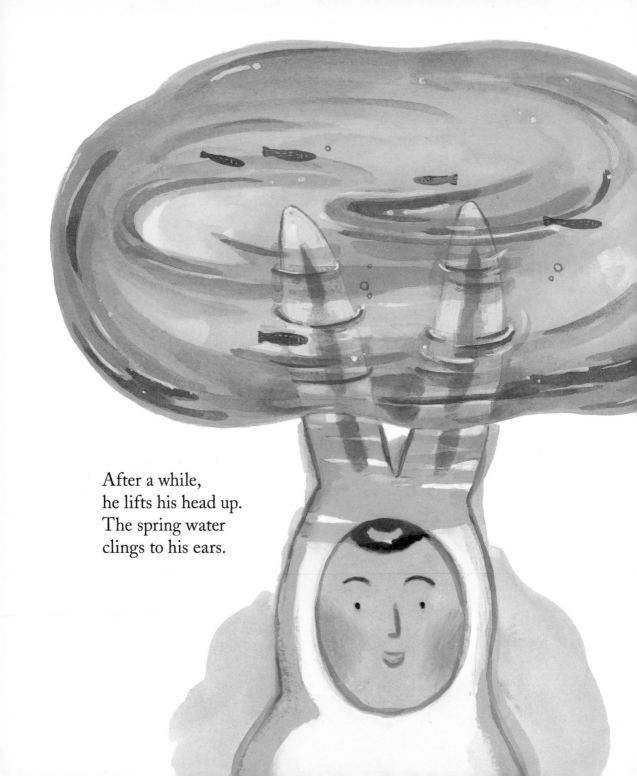

After a while,
he lifts his head up.
The spring water
clings to his ears.

Sato makes a pillow
of the cool spring water
and takes a nap
in the shade of a tree.

When he wakes up later
that night, the moon glimmers
in the spring-water pillow.

Sato reaches in gently
so as not to rouse the
sleeping fish and snacks
on a crisp, cool moon.

A HOLE IN A HAT

There's a tiny hole in
Sato the Rabbit's straw hat.

Peeking carefully
into the hole,

he sees a midsummer forest.
Scree-screech
Keee keee keee
The cicadas are singing.

Peering through once more,
this time he sees

a summer sea.
Splash crash
The waves roar.

He puts his hat back on
and starts walking when
something falls down
with a *plunk* and gets
stuck in the hole.

It's an acorn.

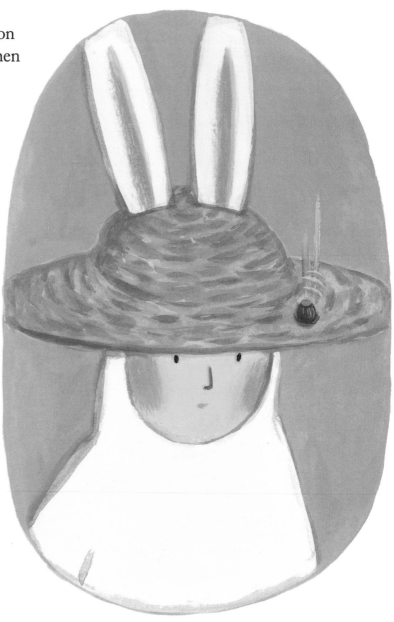

The acorn is stuck tight and won't budge.

Sato tugs at it with all of his might, and …

Pop!
Tumble rumble
Rumble tumble
Whoooooshhhh

Stars, shells, and white sand rush out,
transforming everything in the hole
and everything around Sato into
a crisp autumn day.

The chirping of bugs can be heard
from all around.

*Crick clicka crick
Chirr chirrr chirrrr…*

THE MOON

On a night with a beautiful moon,
Sato the Rabbit goes to a lake deep in a forest.

The moon shimmers on the lake.

Sato puts on his rubber waders
and goes in.

He walks up to the moon
reflecting on the lake.

The moon from the lake is soaking wet,

so Sato dries it out while admiring
the moon in the sky.

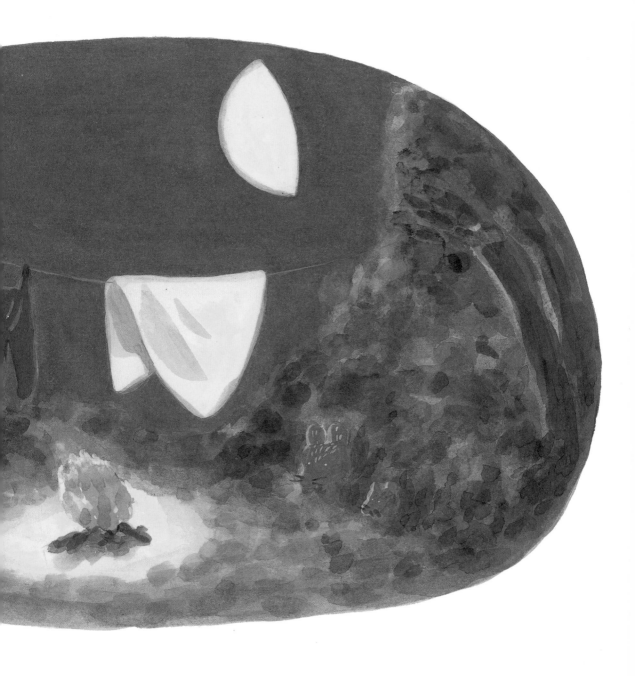

Right around midnight,
the moon is completely dry
and very fluffy.

So, tonight, Sato curls up and sleeps under a moon blanket.

FALLEN LEAVES

One morning,
Sato the Rabbit
walks to the base
of a large tree and
finds that every
leaf has fallen
to the ground.

Sato jumps and rolls
on top of the leaves,
searching for the
fluffiest spot.

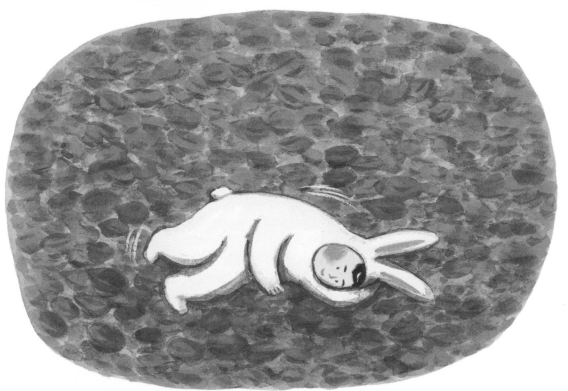

Once he finds it,
he carefully lifts
a corner

and rolls some leaves up.

Sato brings the
rolled-up leaves
to a wedding.

After the couple
walks down the
aisle, Sato rolls
up the leaves
once more
and stands
them on end.

He hooks
a string in
the middle.

Fhhwiipppppp

The wind blows.
Flitter flutter flitter flutter

The leaves blow about above everyone,
on and on and on. ♡

www.enchantedlion.com

First English-language edition published in 2021 by Enchanted Lion Books,
248 Creamer Street, Studio 4, Brooklyn, NY 11231

USAGI NO SATOKUN - TSUKIYO by Yuki AINOYA
Original Japanese edition published by SHOGAKUKAN.
English translation rights arranged with SHOGAKUKAN
through Japan Uni Agency, Inc.

ISBN 978-1-59270-306-7

Printed in Italy by Società Editoriale Grafiche AZ
First Printing